The story of Santa's Snelves

By Michael Bryant   Illustrated by ER Clarke

ISBN: 979-8-9920359-0-2

For my favorite Snelves—
Lisa, Helen, and Mary.
You inspire me, challenge
me, and fill our lives with
endless mischief and joy.
Thank you for keeping
the magic alive.

This story is unique, one you've never heard before.
It's about Santa and his helpers, the ones we adore.

Well, it's Elves of course, but did you know
There are others called Snelves that cook, clean, and sew?

Elves make the toys for good girls and boys,
While Snelves tend the North Pole without many joys.

These Snelves never question their tasks or their lot;
They just follow Santa's orders and do as they ought.

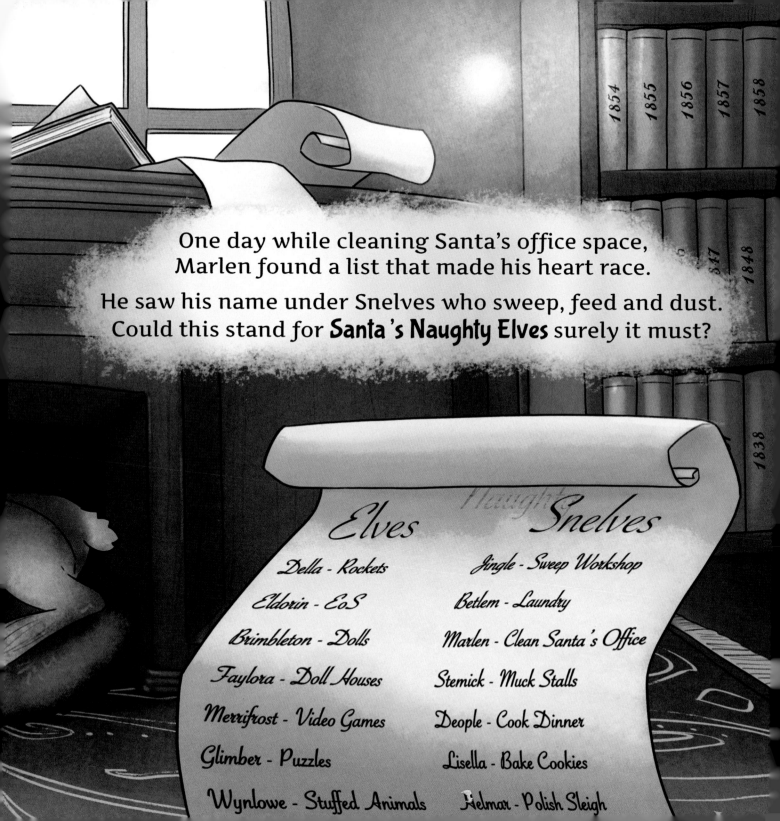

One day while cleaning Santa's office space,
Marlen found a list that made his heart race.

He saw his name under Snelves who sweep, feed and dust.
Could this stand for **Santa's Naughty Elves** surely it must?

Elves

Della - Rockets

Eldorin - EoS

Brimbleton - Dolls

Faylora - Doll Houses

Merrifrost - Video Games

Glimber - Puzzles

Wynlowe - Stuffed Animals

Snelves

Jingle - Sweep Workshop

Betlem - Laundry

Marlen - Clean Santa's Office

Stemick - Muck Stalls

Deople - Cook Dinner

Lisella - Bake Cookies

Helmar - Polish Sleigh

1854 1855 1856 1857 1858

1847 1848

1838

Feeling quite angry,
Marlen gathered the Snelves.
They schemed and planned, very
proud of themselves.

Some would sneak onto Santa's
sleigh on Christmas Eve night
And cause mischief around the
world, much to their delight.

As Santa was busy spreading
Christmas cheer galore,
The Snelves were up to no good,
spreading flour on the floor.

They rearranged decorations and
filled stockings with odds and ends,
Hung ornaments upside down from
where they had been.

They swapped bulbs on Christmas lights with those of lamps and toys, Changed wreaths on windows and doors, anything to annoy.

The snowman in the yard was dressed in summer clothes. What happened to the wrapped gifts? The Snelves took the bows!

In the kitchen, they played,
eating cake and salting the roast beef.
Nothing was safe, not even Grandpa's teeth.

Just when you thought their
naughty tasks were complete,
They put slime in the slippers
meant for Mommy's feet.

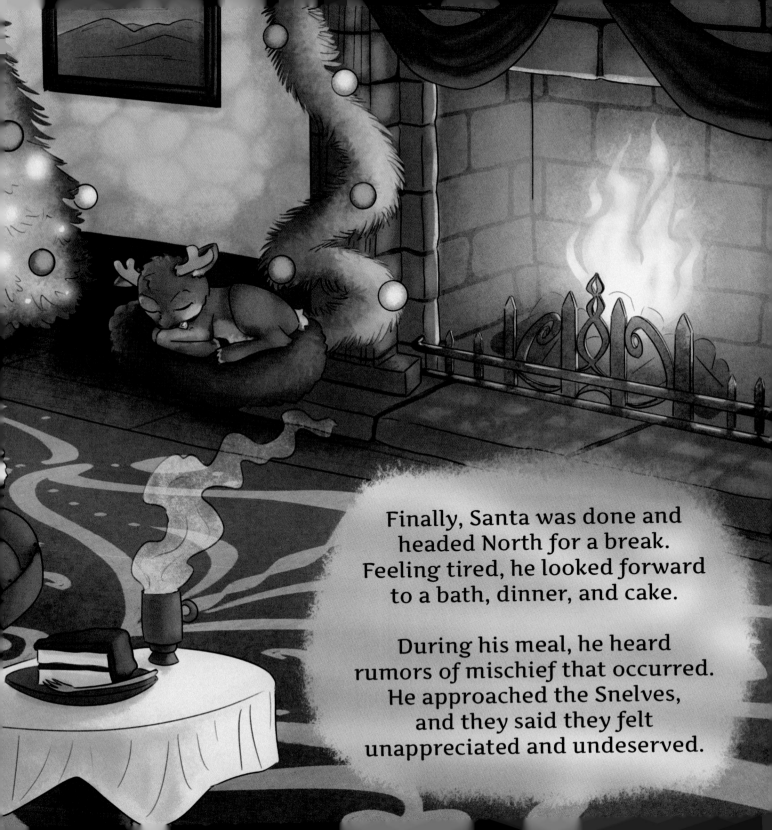

Finally, Santa was done and headed North for a break. Feeling tired, he looked forward to a bath, dinner, and cake.

During his meal, he heard rumors of mischief that occurred. He approached the Snelves, and they said they felt unappreciated and undeserved.

Santa gathered the Snelves to
thank them for all they do
And said, "Without you, my
workshop would have no glue."

He reminded them, "No one is
better and all my Elves are key.
Each of you brings special gifts,
and you all help me."

Now Snelves and
Elves all understood
That each one contributes
to the greater good.

If during your holiday time something's awry,
Thank a mischievous Snelf with a wink and a sigh.

For each of us has a gift to share.
Together, we make a world full of care.

Be grateful for the roles we play
And celebrate our strengths every day.

For everywhere you look, it's clear to see,
We all belong, both you and me.

ael Bryant
e tech guy,
r, author,
ull-time
father.

larke
r, artist
r of many
and
nds.

Made in the USA
Middletown, DE
04 December 2024